THE NEW BABY

BY: DA BUTLER

Mommy says a baby is coming
I'm not sure what that means.
Everyone is excited to meet
him, so it seems

Grandma comes to visit, she
says I'm a lucky girl.
She picks me up and holds me
tight and does a little twirl.

You're going to be a great big sister, she whispers in my ear. I wonder when I'll meet him, how long until he's here?

Mommy's tummy is big and round,
she says it won't be long.
She has to go away for a while
and told me to be strong.

Daddy woke me early today and
said my baby brother is here.
I'm so excited to meet him and
hold him very near

My baby brother is small and sweet
he sleeps all day and night.
I hear him cry from far away
and wake to find my light.

Mommy says he's hungry
or just needs to feel her near.
Sometimes I wish she'd sit with me
she's never really here.

Grandma came to see me
she said you look a little sad.
Are you missing some attention
from your busy mom and your dad?

She said my brother is small and weak
and needs some extra care.
One day he'll grow a little bigger,
big enough to share

Mommy sat beside me
my little brother in her arms.
She said she knows he loves me
and that I'll keep him safe from harm.

I will always protect him.
Little brother I love you.
And when you grow up big and strong,
I know you'll love me too

I will tell you all my secrets
and share my coolest toy.
I'm glad you came to live with me,
you're my favorite little boy

www.ingramcontent.com/pod-product-compliance
Lightning Source LLC
Chambersburg PA
CBHW041438010526
44118CB00002B/111